# MARKET DAY

BY EVE BUNTING

PICTURES BY

HOLLY BERRY

JOANNA COTLER BOOKS
*AN IMPRINT OF HARPERCOLLINSPUBLISHERS*

Market Day
Text copyright © 1996 by Edward D. Bunting and Anne E. Bunting,
Trustees of the Edward D. Bunting and Anne E. Bunting Family Trust.
Illustrations copyright © 1996 by Holly Berry
Printed in the U.S.A. All rights reserved.
Library of Congress Cataloging-in-Publication Data
Bunting, Eve, date
    Market Day / by Eve Bunting ; pictures by Holly Berry.
        p.      cm.
    "Joanna Cotler Books"
    Summary: Tess and Wee Boy observe the farm animals, wonder at the sword-
swallower, hear playing of pipes, and experience all the excitement of a country
fair in Ireland.
    ISBN 0-06-025364-9. — ISBN 0-06-025368-1 (lib. bdg.)
    [1. Markets—Fiction.    2. Fairs—Fiction.    3. Ireland—Fiction.]    I. Berry, Holly, ill.
II. Title.
PZ7.B91527Mar    1996      95-5604
[E]—dc20   CIP   AC
Typography by Christine Kettner
1  2  3  4  5  6  7  8  9  10
❖
First Edition

For my father
And memories of market days
—E. B.

For Chris
—H. B.

The first Thursday of every month is Market Day.

Soon as I waken, I rush downstairs. My father is already eating his breakfast. He gives me the tops of his two boiled eggs. One's white. One's brown. My father says when a hen's in love her egg has a brown shell and that's why brown eggs taste so good.

"What are you going to buy today?" I ask him.

"Pigs, Tess. If the price is right."

He gives me my Market Day penny. "And what are you going to buy?"

"You're not to get sweeties," my mother says. "Last Market Day you were sicker than a cormorant."

"I never buy the same thing twice," I tell her, and gobble my porridge fast. My friend Wee Boy is meeting me at the sweetie stall at nine. He's going to be buying.

Outside, the street is already filled with horses and cows and sheep and goats and farmers and dogs. Stalls line the footpath. Here's the Donegal Lace Woman and here's the Tinker with his pots and pans.

"I'll mend your pots as good as new.
I'll mend your pan and griddle, too."

"Sweet clover honey," the Honey Man calls. The white, waxy honeycombs are piled in front of him. "Here, Tess," he says, and he gives me a broken piece for free.

"Oh, thank you!" The honey tastes of the flowers the bees drank from, and the wax is as thick in your mouth as chewing gum.

Baba-Ali, the sword swallower, is spreading his rug in the town square.

I push through the early crowds for a quick look. Cows and horses and sheep are pushing, too, but the nippy dogs won't let them near, and the handler boys shout: "Back off, you rascals!" They tap at noses with their blackthorn sticks. The sheep have blobs of paint on their wool— red for Gilroy's, blue for O'Leary's, yellow for Doherty's. That's so the buyers will know whose sheep are whose. Sheep faces are all the same. Like daisies.

Baba-Ali has his head back in swallowing position. The long, evil blade glitters.

"Twenty pennies in the hat before he starts swallowing," his helper calls with the hat held out. "One slip of Baba-Ali's hand, and he'll cut his own throat like a turkey gizzard."

People dig out their pennies.

"Silence now!"

There's absolute silence as the sword disappears, inch by inch.

The hat makes the circle again. "Twenty pennies to see it come back up."

Pennies clink.

We're hoping something interesting will appear on the point. But that sword comes up clean as a whistle. It always does.

Old Paddy Mahoney is playing
the pipes on the corner. His hat has four
pennies and a ha'penny in it. On the other
corner is the organ grinder and his
monkey, Nuts. They're doing better. If you
give Nuts a penny, he'll somersault while
the organ handle turns and turns and the
music spills out. I'm sorry for old Paddy,
who has no monkey and could never turn
a somersault himself. I put a penny in his
hat and take out a ha'penny change.
Paddy nods and I nod back. Maybe
someday he'll have enough pennies to
buy himself a monkey.

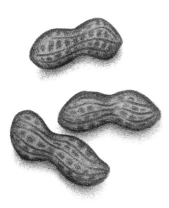

There's my friend Wee Boy in front of Harry Hooey's sweetie stall.

"Hello," I say.

"Hello, Tess," Wee Boy answers.

There are bottles of gob stoppers, big as billiard balls. There are bull's-eyes, clove rock, cherry lips, belly busters, and dolly's mixtures lined up on the stall. Wee Boy has to stand on his tiptoes to get a look at them. He's seven, same as me, but he never grew past four. People say when he's old he'll still be called Wee Boy.

"What will it be, darlin'?" Mrs. Hooey asks.

I shake my head. "Nothing for me. Wee Boy's buying today."

"I'll take a penny poke of gob stoppers," Wee Boy says.

He offers me one and we walk on together.

My father's in the street in a wallow of pigs. They're all scrubbed up and prettied pink for Market Day. I don't go over to him, for he has on his big black rubber Wellington boots, and Wee Boy and I don't. By now you can't walk in the street without your Wellies, what with all those horses and cows and sheep and goats and pigs—and what they've been doing.

My father and the farmer shake on it. The deal's made. I eye the squealing pigs, take out my gob stopper so I can talk, and say, "Some of those pigs are going to be ours."

Wee Boy nods. "They're a fine-looking bunch."

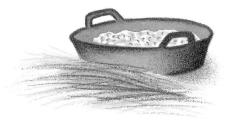

We notice the chicken house and stop for a look.

The chicken house has doors and windows and even a chest of drawers. You can look in the windows and see the hens clucking on their perches. If one clucks out an egg, it goes down a slide into one of the drawers. There are three brown eggs in there already. I wonder which of the hens are in love.

"I could live in a wee house like that if I never be bigger." Wee Boy sounds so sad.

"You'll be bigger," I tell him.

There's a bit of a commotion over by the churchyard. One of the goats got away and stole Mrs. McAfee's petticoat off her clothesline and dragged it back to the square. He had the double frill eaten half off before he was caught. But Mrs. McAfee's a good sport. "Goats will be goats," she says. I've observed that people are less crabby on Market Day.

Wee Boy and I wander on to watch Jehosophat walk on his red-hot coals. He wears a white turban and short trousers made from a flour bag. Long trousers would burn on the bottom. Sometimes Jehosophat shows us the soles of his feet. They're like corrugated paper. Once he boiled water on his coals and passed around mugs of tea. He even had sugar.

The gypsy caravans have been pulled onto the footpath. Madame Savanna is sitting in front of the one that's painted over with moons and stars.

"Tell your fortunes, lovies," she calls out. Once in a while Madame lets us look in her crystal ball, but she de-magics it first. De-magicking wipes out the future so all you can see is yourself and maybe a funny-looking cow behind you. My mother says Madame Savanna makes up what people want to hear.

"You mean she tells lies?" I ask.

"No," my mother says. "She has a clever way with words. People have to go through things, and sometimes it's the hope that keeps them going."

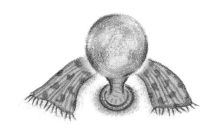

I have an idea.

"Wee Boy," I say. "Get your fortune told."

"Naw. I spent my penny on gob stoppers."

"I have a ha'penny." I put it in Madame's hand. "Tell Wee Boy his future."

She waves him to her stool on the other side of the crystal ball.

"I see *you*, Wee Boy, and you're a fine figure of a gentleman, smart at business and strong of heart," she says.

"Am I big?" Wee Boy whispers.

"Big and brave as you'll ever need to be."

Wee Boy sits taller in the stool. He's smiling all over his face. I'm glad I spent my ha'penny.

Wee Boy and I stay together all day, and it's a great day. Especially as a good rain comes down just as everybody's leaving, and it cleans off the street so the townspeople don't have to do it.

Wee Boy and I aren't sad a bit. Won't it be Market Day all over again on the first Thursday of next month?

"Cherry lips next time," I tell Wee Boy. "I'm buying."

Wee Boy nods. "Cherry lips."

**We shake on it.**